Piglette

by Katelyn Aronson

pictures by Eva Byrne

VIKING

On a farm in France, Piglette arrived last in her litter and dainty as a daisy.

"The seventh!" said her mother.

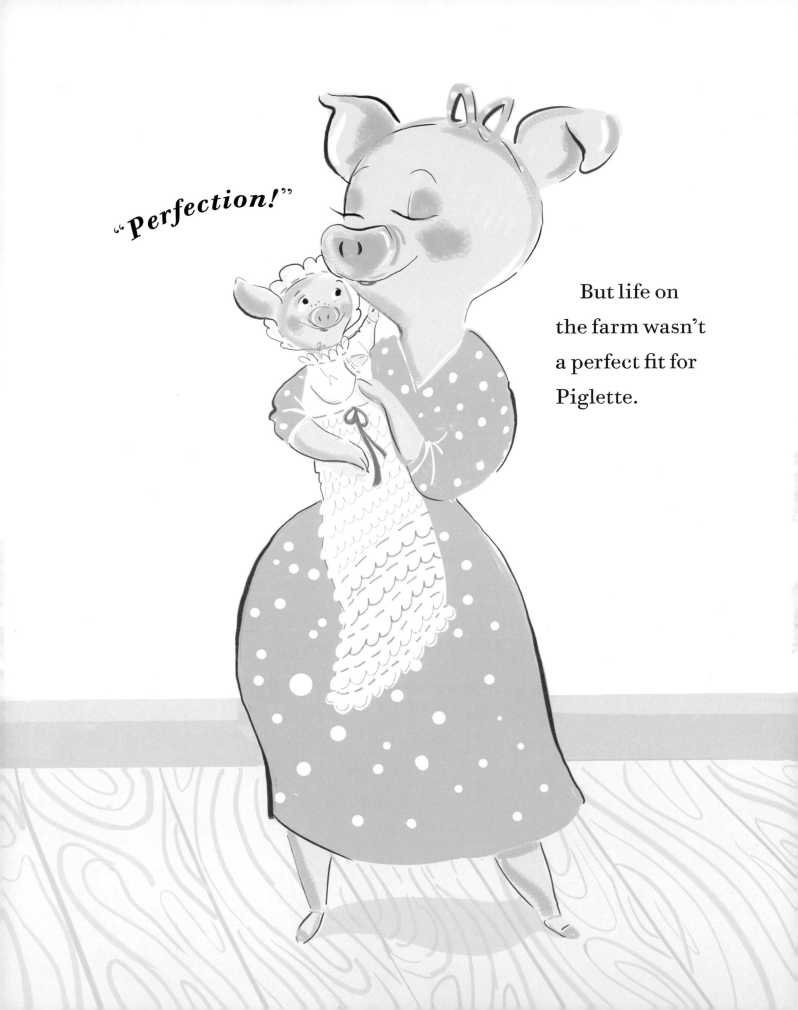

"Perfection!"

But life on
the farm wasn't
a perfect fit for
Piglette.

Nothing piggish seemed to please her.

She snorted at her slop. **"P-U!"**

"Persnickety," said her brothers.

While the others played, Piglette pampered herself.

"*Prissy!*"
said her sisters.

So sometimes, she escaped to the one place she preferred . . .

The pasture.

There, in the open air, she closed her eyes and breathed deeply, catching the scents of the trees and blossoms. She memorized the perfume of every posy she picked—*Lily. Lilac. Lavender. Rose*—and spent hours making crowns of flowers.

It came as no surprise when, one day, a pungent pickup piqued her curiosity. . . .

Piglette packed her bags. She kissed her family farewell and departed for Paris.

"The seventh!"
her mother sobbed.
Perfection!

"*Paris!*" whispered Piglette. . . .

"*What* will I do here? *Who* will I be?"

Piglette the poet?

Piglette the painter?

Piglette the pastry chef?

Perfectly pleasant pastimes, but Piglette
sensed she had something more in store.

That's when she happened upon the
perfumery of Madame Paradee.

Inside, the air
smelled like a field
of flowers.

Piglette sampled.

Sniff. "Mmmm. Peony."

Sniff. "Primrose."

Sniff. "Sweet pea."

"And this?" asked Madame Paradee.

Sniff. "Hmmm . . . Honeysuckle?" said Piglette.

"Ooh-la-la! You are just the snout I am looking for, my petite!" said Madame Paradee. "You start work tomorrow!"

The perfumery became Piglette's paradise.
She learned every fragrance by snout.

She knew which ones
could pep you up,

calm you down,

or even make you
fall in love.

Madame Paradee threw important parties with poets,
painters, and pianists. They brought presents and pastries.

They pampered Piglette like a princess.

Perhaps I've found my place! thought Piglette.

And yet . . .

Sometimes the sights, the sounds, the
smells of the city grew . . . smothering.

P-U! "Please! Don't push!" said Piglette.

She wandered the streets, searching for escape, until at last . . .

A park.

There, in the open air, Piglette closed her eyes and breathed deeply, catching the scents of the trees and flowers.

A strange wind whispered
from far away. *Whoooooooooosh* came
whiffs of grass and mud, horse and hay—the countryside.
 Piglette pictured her mother, three brothers, and three
sisters. Tears trickled down her snout, one for each of them.
 "Seven," she sighed. *"Perfection."*

Piglette packed her bags. She pecked
Madame Paradee on each cheek. . . .
"It's been heaven here,
but I have to go home. . . ."

Soon the long-lost fragrance of the countryside hung all around her.

"My Piglette!" cried her mother.

Her brothers and sisters came running to greet her.

The pasture was my place all along, she thought.

And yet . . .

She missed the city.
How can I bring a bit of
Paris to the pasture?
Piglette pondered.

Then . . . she knew!
She set to planning a
party of her own.

She sent postcards to Madame Paradee and all her friends.

The day her guests arrived, she
gathered her family, too. They'd never
once suspected her surprise . . .

"*Voilà!*" Piglette proclaimed.

She'd prepared rose petal dips and mud masks for her city friends. Perfumes and bubble baths for her family. Picnics of pastries. Flower crowns for one and all.

Everything and everyone Piglette loved gathered into one fragrant bouquet. And it smelled divine.

"Pictuuure . . . !"
CLICK.

"Perfection."

For Bee —K.A.

For my family, with love —E.B.

VIKING

An imprint of Penguin Random House LLC, New York

First published in the United States of America by Viking,

an imprint of Penguin Random House LLC, 2020

Visit us online at penguinrandomhouse.com

LIBRARY OF CONGRESS CATALOGING-IN-PUBLICATION DATA IS AVAILABLE

ISBN 9780593116784

1 3 5 7 9 10 8 6 4 2

Manufactured in China   Book design by Nancy Brennan   Set in Bodoni Six